A Gift For

From

How to Use Your Interactive Story Buddy™:

1. Activate your Story Buddy™ by pressing the "On / Off" button on the ear.
2. Read the story aloud in a quiet place. Speak in a clear voice when you see the highlighted phrases.
3. Listen to your Story Buddy™ respond with several different phrases throughout the book.

Clarity and speed of reading affect the way Bell responds. She may not always respond to young children.

Watch for even more interactive Story Buddy™ characters. For more information, visit us on the Web at Hallmark.com/StoryBuddy.

I Reply ™ TECHNOLOGY Hallmark's **I Reply Technology** brings your Story Buddy™ to life! When you read the key phrases out loud, your Story Buddy™ gives a variety of responses, so each time you read feels as magical as the first.

BOOK 1

Bell's Big Move

By Tom Shay-Zapien

Hallmark
GIFT BOOKS

There are lots of lovable puppies in the world, but of
all the little puppies anyone could possibly know, there was
probably none as lovable as Bell.

She had style, charm, and flair. She even had a fancy little
collar. There was no denying it, Bell was one pretty puppy!

Bell lived in a beautiful house in Palm City and had everything a puppy could possibly want—plus a few extras. She was neat, tidy, and well-mannered, but most of all, she was loved by Sofia.

Bell and Sofia did everything together. They strolled by the school and played in the park. They went shopping downtown. And every Saturday, they strolled to the Palm City Café for biscotti and tea.

On this Saturday, the café owner gave Bell a fancy little treat. Sofia grinned and adjusted the collar on her puppy. "Bell, can you say thank you?"

As soon as they finished at the café, it was time for the puppy salon. This was Bell's favorite place.

"Up you go, Bell!" Sofia said, lifting her onto the table. "It's time to get beautiful!"

When Bell's hair was all brushed, her nails were all clipped, and her ribbon was tied in a perfect bow, it was time to go home. When they got there, Sofia's parents had some news. They told her they were going to move.

"We have to move *where*?" Sofia cried. "And so *soon*?" Seeing Sofia upset did not make Bell very happy.

Saying good-bye to their friends was even harder than Sofia had imagined.

"I'm going to miss you so much," said Megan as she scratched Bell on the tummy.

Emily gave the little pup a great big hug and said, "I love you, Bell."

When they arrived in Pineville, Sofia couldn't help but notice how different everything was. There were no tall buildings or busy streets or crowded walkways.

"It'll never be Palm City, that's for sure," Sofia said. "But at least my best friend is right here with me." Sofia gave Bell a long hug.

And that's when Sofia noticed—Bell's fancy collar was gone! How long had it been missing? Where could it be? Would they ever find it? This did not make Bell very happy.

Suddenly, Bell heard a jingling sound. She jumped out
of Sofia's arms and dashed through the snow to follow it.

"Somebody sure likes the sound of your collar," a boy
said to his dog.

"Her name is Bell," Sofia said. "And I'm Sofia. We just
moved here."

"Oh, hi! I'm Andrew. And this is Jingle. Welcome to Pineville!"

"Thanks," said Sofia. "Bell, can you say thank you?"

Sofia shivered. "Is it always this cold here?"

"Only in the wintertime," said Andrew. "But there's still lots of fun stuff to do. Especially on Saturdays. If you want, Jingle and I can show you around."

"We'd like that," Sofia said.

"See you tomorrow then!" said Andrew, as Jingle barked good-bye to his new friends.

The very next day, Andrew and Jingle took their
new neighbors to all their favorite places. They strolled
by the school and played at the park. It almost made
Sofia forget that they couldn't find Bell's collar anywhere.

Then they went to Pineville Bakery. When the owner found out Sofia and Bell had just moved into town, he treated them all to hot cocoa and cookies!

"These are so delicious!" Sofia said between bites. Then she shared a little piece with Bell. "Bell, can you say thank you?"

PET SHOP

As soon as they finished at the bakery, Andrew
led the way to the pet shop, where Sofia and Bell met
Jingle's groomer. She patted Bell on the head and said,
"Bell, you're such a pretty puppy!"

"A pretty girl like you should have a pretty collar," said the groomer. "We just got some new ones in this morning."

"Should we get one?" Sofia asked. "They are very pretty."

Jingle pawed at one with a shiny bell, just like his. It was perfect.

That night in their new bed, Bell's collar rang sweetly as Sofia talked about all the good things that happened that day. The new places. The new collar. But they both agreed the best part of all was making new friends. And that made Bell smile.

Did you have fun with Bell and Sofia?
We would love to hear from you!

Please send your comments to:

Hallmark Book Feedback

P.O. Box 419034

Mail Drop 215

Kansas City, MO 64141

Or e-mail us at:

booknotes@hallmark.com